Secret
PRINCESSES

With special thanks to Anne Marie Ryan
For everyone who has ever had a best friend.

ORCHARD BOOKS

First published in Great Britain in 2018 by The Watts Publishing Group

1 3 5 7 9 10 8 6 4 2

Text copyright © Hothouse Fiction, 2018
Illustrations copyright © Orchard Books, 2018

A CIP catalogue record for this book
is available from the British Library.

ISBN 978 1 40835 115 4

Printed and bound in Great Britain by Clays Ltd, Elcograf S.p.A

The paper and board used in this book are made from wood from responsible sources.

Orchard Books
An imprint of
Hachette Children's Group
Part of The Watts Publishing Group Limited
Carmelite House
50 Victoria Embankment
London EC4Y 0DZ

An Hachette UK Company
www.hachette.co.uk
www.hachettechildrens.co.uk

Series created by Hothouse Fiction

Secret PRINCESSES

Princess Prom

ROSIE BANKS

Wishing Star Palace

The Secret Princess Promise

"I promise that I will be kind and brave,

Using my magic to help and save,

Granting wishes and doing my best,

To make people smile and bring happiness."

Story One

CHAPTER ONE
Advent Adventure

"Deck the halls with boughs of holly, fa la la la la, LA LA LA LA!"

"Yay!" Charlotte Williams clapped proudly as her dad and the town choir sang the last notes of the Christmas carol. The choir was performing at the school Christmas fair. The school hall wasn't decked with boughs of holly, but it was decorated with paper snowflakes and glittery stars that Charlotte and the other pupils had made in art lessons. It looked so Christmassy that Charlotte barely recognised it as the place where she and her classmates normally had assemblies and PE lessons.

"That was great, Dad," said Charlotte, running over to give her father a hug.

"Your choir should go on *Talent Quest*," said Liam, Charlotte's younger brother.

"Yeah! You might win, like Alice," said Harvey, Liam's twin.

Dad chuckled. "I'm no Alice de Silver."

Alice de Silver had become a pop star after winning the television competition *Talent Quest*. But before she got famous, Alice had been Charlotte's babysitter!

"Who wants a hot chocolate?" asked Charlotte's mum. "My treat."

"Can we have marshmallows?" asked Liam.

"And whipped cream?" said Harvey.

"Absolutely," said Mum, grinning.

"Is it OK if I do some Christmas shopping instead?" asked Charlotte. "I want to find a present for Mia." Even though Christmas was still a few weeks away, Charlotte wanted to make sure her best friend's gift arrived before the twenty-fifth of December. It took a long time for parcels to get from California, where Charlotte's family lived, to England, where Mia lived.

"Good idea," said her mum.

Charlotte browsed through stalls selling silky scarves, scented candles and chocolate truffles. She lingered in front of a stall selling ornaments shaped like animals. There were dogs, cats, bears and dolphins – and even a unicorn! *Which one would Mia like best*, wondered Charlotte. It was hard to choose just one because Mia loved ALL animals equally!

Charlotte moved on to a stall selling
jewellery. Silver rings, bracelets and necklaces
were arranged around a mirror.

"I love your necklace," said the jewellery
lady. "Where did you get it?"

"Oh," said Charlotte, glancing down at
her necklace with its
gold half-heart
pendant. "Er,
a friend gave
it to me." She
couldn't tell
the lady that
the friend was
Alice de Silver – and
that the necklace was magic!

Alice wasn't just a famous singer. She was also a Secret Princess, who used magic to grant wishes. Shortly before Charlotte's family had moved to California, Alice had given Charlotte and Mia matching necklaces and invited them to train to become Secret Princesses like her.

Since beginning their training, the girls had earned diamond tiaras, ruby slippers that let them travel magically, sapphire rings that warned them when danger was near, and moonstone bracelets that let them call the Secret Princesses. On their last visit to the palace, the girls had even earned special aquamarine combs that let them turn into mermaids. Now they only had one more thing

to earn before becoming Secret Princesses –
their magic wands!

"Are you looking for anything in particular?"
asked the jewellery lady.

"Do you have any earrings?" asked
Charlotte.

The lady showed her some earrings, and
Charlotte chose a pair of delicate silver hoops
for her mum's Christmas present. As she
handed the lady the money, Charlotte caught
a glimpse of herself in the mirror. Her gold
pendant was even shinier than usual – because
it was glowing!

"Thank you!" said Charlotte, taking her
change and hurrying away. She ducked out
of the bustling school hall and into a quiet

corridor. Holding her glowing pendant in her hand, she whispered, "I wish I could see Mia."

Golden light poured out of the pendant, swirling around Charlotte. The magical light swept her away from the Christmas fair – and up to the clouds!

A moment later, Charlotte arrived in the grand entrance hall of Wishing Star Palace, the magical place where the Secret Princesses gathered. Charlotte's clothes had changed into a pretty pink princess dress and she could feel her diamond tiara resting on her curls. Her brown eyes lit up with excitement as she spotted a blonde girl in a gold dress.

"Mia!" she squealed, dashing over to hug her best friend.

"I'm so happy to see you!" said Mia, her blue eyes sparkling.

A Secret Princess with cool red streaks in her strawberry-blonde hair popped her head out of a door down the hall. "In here, girls!" she called, beckoning to Mia and Charlotte.

"Hi, Alice!" cried Mia and Charlotte, hurrying over.

Alice greeted them each with a kiss on the cheek as they came into a cosy sitting room. A roaring fire crackled in the fireplace and Secret Princesses sat around it in comfy armchairs.

"What's this?" asked Charlotte, spotting a model of Wishing Star Palace in front of the fire. It had white walls and four turrets, just like the real palace.

"It's our new advent calendar," explained Princess Alice.

Charlotte and Mia knelt down in front of the model to have a closer look. The doors and heart-shaped windows had numbers on them.

"We each contributed a special gift," explained Princess Sophie, an artist whose pendant was shaped like a paintbrush.

"And we each get to open a door," said Princess Grace, an actor back in the real world.

"We thought one of you girls would like to have the first turn," said Princess Alice.

"You can go first," Charlotte told Mia.

"No, you should go first," insisted Mia.

"I thought this might happen," Alice said, laughing. "Let's go in alphabetical order," she suggested. "Charlotte can open the first door, and Mia can open one on your next visit."

"OK," said Charlotte. "But I'm going to share my gift with Mia."

"I expected nothing less from our future Friendship Princesses," said Alice, winking.

Mia and Charlotte were training to be a very rare and powerful sort of Secret Princess. Friendship Princesses were close friends who always worked together.

"Here goes," said Charlotte, opening a heart-shaped window marked with the number one.

NEIGH! A unicorn made of silvery light galloped out of the window. Charlotte and Mia grinned as it pranced around the room in a shimmering blaze, then vanished into thin air.

"It says
something on
the back of the
window," said
Mia.

Charlotte read
out the words: "A
unicorn ride with
Princess Ella!"

*JINGLE!
JINGLE! JINGLE!*

The sound of
jingling bells came from outside. Charlotte ran
to the window and looked out.

"Mia, come quick!" she called.

Mia joined her by the window and gasped.

Princess Ella waved to them from the frosty palace grounds. But she wasn't alone – there were three snow-white unicorns with her!

CHAPTER TWO
The Christmas Candle

Holding hands, Mia and Charlotte ran through the palace. They burst out of the front door into the chilly night air where Princess Ella and the unicorns were waiting for them.

"Ready to go for a ride?" asked Princess Ella, smiling. Her pawprint-shaped pendant glinted in the moonlight. Ella was a vet and she looked after all of Wishing Star Palace's animals.

"Yes!" cried Mia.

Charlotte shivered and rubbed her arms.

"Are you shivering with cold or excitement?" asked Ella.

"Both," said Charlotte.

Ella waved her wand and suddenly Mia and Charlotte were wearing warm, velvet riding cloaks.

"Thanks," said Charlotte, drawing the cloak around her.

Ella gave Mia a boost on to the first unicorn's back. "This one is called Angel."

"You're gorgeous," Mia said, stroking the unicorn's neck.

Angel whinnied softly, her warm breath puffing out like clouds in the frosty air.

Then Ella helped Charlotte on to a unicorn named Snowy.

"Um, what should I hold on to?" asked Charlotte. None of the unicorns had saddles, bridles or reins.

"Hold Snowy's mane," said Ella, climbing on

to the third unicorn's back. "Hello, Frosty," she said, giving him a pat.

As Charlotte grabbed a handful of Snowy's silky mane, the unicorn pawed the ground with his hooves, eager to be on the move.

Ella tapped Frosty's sides lightly with her heels and all three unicorns set off at a gentle trot. Their pearly horns glowed in the dark night, illuminating the palace's grounds.

"The gardens look so pretty," said Mia. Snow covered the ground, glittering in the moonlight. The shrubs had been trimmed into festive shapes such as snowmen, polar bears and elves. There were two bushes shaped like reindeer, nibbling moss underneath the trees.

"Wait a minute!" cried Charlotte, as one the

reindeer moved. "Those are real reindeer."

"It's Joy and Noelle!" said Mia.

The girls waved to the reindeer. They'd met them on a previous visit to the palace.

The unicorns trotted further into the enormous grounds. The buildings and trees twinkled with white fairy lights. As they passed the greenhouse, the swimming pool and the butterfly garden, Charlotte thought about all the wonderful times they had had exploring the grounds with their princess friends.

"It looks magical," breathed Mia.

"It *is* magical," giggled Charlotte.

"You know what I mean," said Mia. "Even more magical than usual."

"I agree," said Princess Ella, smiling. "Wishing Star Palace is never more beautiful than at Christmastime."

Snow began to fall in fluffy flurries. Charlotte held out her hand to try and catch a snowflake. Suddenly, she heard a faint voice. It was coming from her moonstone bracelet.

"Hello," she said, holding the jewel close to her ear.

"Can you come back now?" came Princess Sylvie's voice from the bracelet. "It's almost time for the ceremony."

"We need to get back," Charlotte told the others. "There's a ceremony starting soon."

"To the palace!" cried Ella.

NEIGH! The unicorns whinnied and began

to gallop through the snow.

"Whee!" called Charlotte, clutching Snowy's mane. Cold air rushed against her cheeks as the unicorns raced back.

When they reached the palace, Charlotte swung her leg over Snowy's back and hopped down to the ground.

"Thanks for the ride," she said, stroking Snowy's smooth horn. The unicorn nuzzled her with his velvety nose.

As the unicorns trotted back to the palace stables, Ella and the girls went inside. The Secret Princesses stood in the entrance hall, in front of a huge Christmas tree.

"Did you enjoy your ride?" asked Princess Alice, helping the girls take their cloaks off.

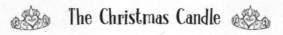

"It was awesome!" said
Charlotte, rubbing her hands
in front of the fireplace to warm
them up. In the gold-framed
mirror above the fireplace she
could see that her cheeks were
rosy. On the mantel was a white
candle, surrounded by a wreath

of pine and bright red holly berries.

"That's a pretty candle," said Mia, joining Charlotte by the fire.

"It's the reason we called you back," said Princess Sylvie. "We're going to light our new Christmas Candle."

"What does it do?" asked Mia.

"This year we're going to combine our Christmas magic," explained Princess Anna, who was the oldest and wisest Secret Princess. "That way we can make Christmas Day merry and bright for everyone."

"With every Christmas wish we grant, the candle will shine even brighter," added Sylvie, "spreading Christmas joy far and wide."

The Secret Princesses dimmed the lights and

gathered around the hearth. They all took out their wands and pointed them at the candle. Together, the princesses said the magic words:

While this candle glows with magical light,
We'll make this Christmas merry and bright!

Sparkling light shot out of the wands. The golden beams joined together, lighting the candle. The Christmas Candle's bright flame flickered and danced, filling the whole room with its warm glow.

"Wow!" breathed Mia. "I can't wait until I have a magic wand."

Charlotte squeezed her best friend's hand.

"It won't be much longer, girls," said Alice. "You've completed every stage of your training. Now you just need to grant a double Christmas wish and you'll be full Secret Princesses!"

Mia and Charlotte exchanged excited looks, their eyes shining in the candlelight.

WHOOSH!

A gust of icy wind blasted out of the fireplace.

"Brrr!" said Charlotte.

The cold air swirled around the room like a tornado. It spun around the Christmas Candle and – *POOF* – snuffed out the flame!

"Oh no!" gasped Alice. "The Christmas Candle's gone out."

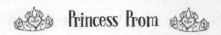

A face appeared in the mirror above the fireplace. Black hair with a white streak framed sharp cheekbones and cruel green eyes.

"Princess Poison!" Mia gasped.

Princess Poison had once been a Secret Princess, but she'd been banished from the palace for using wishes to get more power instead of helping other people. Ever since then, she'd used her magic to spoil people's wishes and make trouble for the Secret Princesses.

"I won't say Happy Christmas," said Princess Poison smugly. "Because it won't be – for anyone."

"Don't you dare spoil Christmas!" said Charlotte, glaring at Princess Poison.

"I hope you didn't wish for a magic wand for Christmas," said Princess Poison, smirking nastily. "Because you definitely won't be getting one. The two of you will NEVER

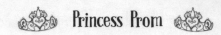

become Secret Princesses."

Then, as quickly as it had appeared, her glowering face vanished.

CHAPTER THREE
A Double Wish

A curl of smoke drifted up from the candle's wick, filling the entrance hall with a burnt smell. It wasn't just the candle's light that had gone out of the room – the feeling of Christmas joy had also disappeared. The Secret Princesses' faces were full of despair.

"Don't worry," Charlotte comforted Mia, seeing the tears in her friend's eyes. "We'll get

our wands. Princess Poison won't stop us."

Shaking her head, Mia brushed away her tears. "I'm just upset because Princess Poison is trying to ruin Christmas."

"Can you light the candle again?" Charlotte asked Alice hopefully.

Alice shook her head sadly. "I'm afraid not. The reason that the candle is so powerful is that the Secret Princesses have combined all their Christmas magic."

"The only way to get more magic is to grant more Christmas wishes," said Princess Anna.

"We'll help!" exclaimed Mia.

"We don't have very long," said Sylvie. "We'll need to grant a lot of Christmas wishes to make enough magic to relight the candle before Christmas Day."

"We can do it," said Charlotte, "if we all work together."

The Secret Princesses nodded, suddenly looking a lot more cheerful.

"Quick!" said Mia. "Let's check the Christmas tree!"

The enormous pine tree was decorated with colourful lights and shiny baubles. Whenever anyone made a Christmas wish, their face appeared in the baubles.

"Look!" cried Mia. "Someone's made a Christmas wish!"

But there wasn't just one face in the baubles' shiny surface – there were two! One girl was short, with a blonde bob and wide hazel eyes.

The taller girl had long, brown hair which she wore in pigtails.

"It's a double wish!" exclaimed Charlotte. Turning to Alice, she said, "Please can we grant it?"

"Of course," said Alice.

Charlotte grinned at Mia. "You know what this means? If we grant both wishes, we'll help relight the candle – AND earn our wands!"

Mia and Charlotte held a bauble in their hands. The girls' faces were replaced by the names "Shelley" and "Kat".

"Are you ready to save Christmas?" Charlotte asked Mia.

Mia nodded, eyes shining with determination.

"Good luck!"
shouted
the Secret
Princesses.

"Shelley!"
said Mia.

"Kat!" said
Charlotte.

Magical light

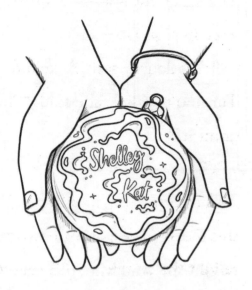

swirled out of the bauble and carried Mia and
Charlotte away from the palace. They landed
in a corridor lined with metal lockers.

"We must be in a school," said Charlotte,
looking around. There were posters on the wall
advertising a bake sale, and another that said
'Jinglebell Prom' in sparkly letters.

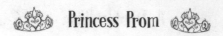

"Uh-oh," said Mia, glancing down.
"I hope we don't get in trouble for not
wearing uniforms." Their princess outfits
had disappeared, and now the girls were
wearing jolly Christmas jumpers. Mia's had a
reindeer on it, with a red pom-pom for a nose.
Charlotte's had a candy cane decorated with
sparkly red and white sequins.

Just then, the two girls who'd made the double Christmas wish came out of a classroom. Shelley and Kat were wearing Christmas jumpers, too!

Phew! thought Charlotte.

"Hi," said Shelley, the shorter girl with a neat blonde bob. "Are you volunteers for the bake sale?"

"Yes!" said Charlotte quickly. "I'm Charlotte and this is Mia."

"Nice jumpers," said Kat, the tall girl with dark hair. She had earrings shaped like little presents and a Christmas tree on her jumper. "I'm Kat and this is Shelley. We're organising the Jinglebell Prom."

"It's great that so many people wore Christmas jumpers today," said Shelley, whose

sweater had a snowman on it. "Everyone who did made a donation so we raised a lot of money for the prom."

As they followed Kat and Shelley down the hallway, Mia whispered to Charlotte, "What's a prom?"

"It's a school dance," Charlotte whispered back. "A really fancy one. They're popular in America."

In the school hall, Mia and Charlotte helped Shelley and Kat set up the tables for the bake sale. They spread tablecloths on top and set out the treats people had donated.

"Yum!" said Charlotte, putting out a tray of cupcakes with red and green icing. "These look delicious."

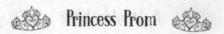

"Not as good as these," said Mia, arranging a plate of gingerbread men.

There were home-made mince pies, cookies shaped like snowmen and slices of fruity Christmas cake. Someone had even made a beautiful chocolate log decorated with meringue mushrooms.

"I really wish we can raise lots of money for the prom today," said Shelley, arranging

biscuits on a stand. "We need to pay for the food, decorations and a DJ."

Mia and Charlotte exchanged a meaningful look. They'd found out what Shelley had wished for!

"It sounds like it will be an amazing night," said Charlotte.

"I really wish it will be a lot of fun," said Kat. "It's the first time our school has ever held a

prom. So I really want it to be a success."

Aha! thought Charlotte. Now they knew
Kat's wish too!

"OK," said Shelley, setting out the last tray
of fairy cakes. "That's everything. Now we just
need people to buy it."

"I'm sure they will," said Charlotte, her
tummy rumbling. She reached out to smooth
down a tablecloth and a blue light caught her
eye. It was coming from her ring!

"Mia!" she whispered urgently. "Our sapphire
rings are flashing!"

Danger was near!

The door opened and a tall woman in a
green dress strode into the school hall. "My,
my," said Princess Poison, clattering across the

wooden floor on spiky high heels. "Doesn't this look scrummy?"

She picked up a cupcake and scooped off some icing with a long-nailed finger. Then she licked the frosting off.

"Hmm," she said. "A bit too sickly sweet for my taste. Just like you two goody-goodies."

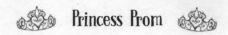

"Hey!" cried Shelley. "You need to buy that."

Princess Poison ignored her. She picked up a gingerbread man and crushed it in her hand. "Get ready for your wishes to CRUMBLE!"

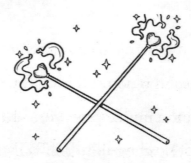

CHAPTER FOUR
Cake Catastrophe!

Princess Poison pulled out her wand. She
pointed it at the table and hissed out a spell:

**Smash every biscuit and ruin each cake.
Not a penny will this bake sale make!**

Green light exploded out of the wand.
Princess Poison's bad magic turned the display

of treats into a horrible mess. The biscuits were burnt, the gingerbread men had lost their arms and legs, and the mince pies were squashed flat as pancakes. The chocolate roll was now an actual log sprouting REAL mushrooms!

BRIIIINNG!

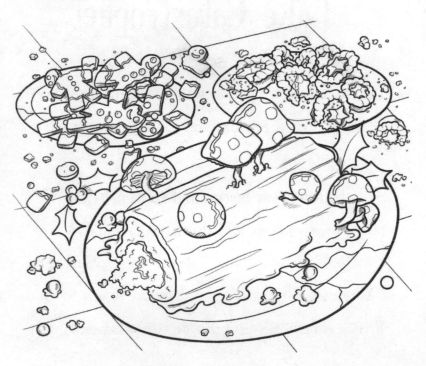

The bell rang loudly. School was finished for the day.

"Oh no!" wailed Kat. "What are we going to do now? Nobody's going to want to buy any of this stuff."

"You're right," said Princess Poison. "I've just lost my appetite!" She waved her wand again and vanished with a flash of green light.

Kat and Shelley goggled at the empty space where Princess Poison had been standing a second before.

"Who was that lady?" asked Shelley. "And how did she do that?"

"There's no time to explain," said Charlotte. "We need to fix this mess."

"But how?" asked Kat. "It's impossible."

Charlotte could hear voices and footsteps coming from outside the hall. Hungry students were on their way to the bake sale.

"No, it's not," she said.

It was time to make a wish!

Mia and Charlotte held their glowing pendants together, the two halves forming a perfect gold heart.

"I wish for a brilliant Christmas bake sale," said Mia.

Golden light beamed out of the heart and on to the table. Magic transformed the crumbling cakes into a delicious display. The table had been replaced with a red wooden sleigh and on top of it cake stands heaved with festive goodies. There were meringues shaped like

snowmen, mini Christmas cakes and chocolate logs, and dainty mince pies dusted with icing sugar. On the wall behind the sleigh, the word PROM was spelled out in doughnuts frosted with silver and gold icing.

"Oh my gosh!" gasped Kat.

Shelley rubbed her eyes. "What just happened?"

"A bit of Christmas magic," Charlotte said with a grin.

"Charlotte and I are training to become Secret Princesses," explained Mia. "We came here to grant your Christmas wishes."

"That mean lady is Princess Poison," added Charlotte. "She's trying to stop us."

Before Kat and Shelley could ask any more

questions, their classmates flooded into the school hall. As Kat and Shelley sold tickets to the prom, Mia and Charlotte looked after the bake sale.

"Oh man," exclaimed a boy, staring at the treats. "I can't decide between a cookie or a mince pie."

"Get both!" suggested Mia. "It's for a good cause, after all."

"Good thinking," said the boy. He handed Mia some money, and Charlotte served him his treats.

"I'll have a doughnut, please," said a girl.

"All the money raised today is going towards the Jinglebell Prom," Charlotte announced to the kids waiting be served.

A lady in a smart suit bought an enormous Christmas cake decorated with marzipan penguins and polar bears.

"Thanks, Miss Murphy!" called Shelley.

"That's our headteacher," Kat whispered to Mia and Charlotte.

Before long, every single treat had been sold. As Mia and Charlotte cleared up the empty cake stands and trays, Kat and Shelley counted the money they'd made.

"We did really well!" exclaimed Kat. "We've made almost enough to book the DJ we want."

"And we sold lots of tickets to the prom," said Shelley.

"Thanks so much for your help," said Kat. "We couldn't have done it without you."

"That's what we're here for," said Charlotte.

"Let us know what else we can do," said Mia.

"Actually," said Shelley, "this evening we have a gift-wrapping fundraiser at the shopping centre. We can head over there once we've tidied up."

As the girls swept the hall and put the rubbish in bin bags, a short, tubby man came into the hall.

"Sorry!" called Kat. "The bake sale's over."

But Mia and Charlotte knew the man didn't want to buy cakes. He was Princess Poison's assistant, Hex, and he only wanted one thing – to cause trouble!

"I don't need
cake," Hex said,
with a creepy smile.
"I'm sweet enough
already."

"Go away," Mia
told him.

"Not until I've
done what I came
here to do," said
Hex. "And that's spoil a wish!"

"Don't you ever get tired of doing Princess
Poison's dirty work?" asked Charlotte, sighing.
"Do you like being bad?"

Not bothering to reply, Hex marched over to
the rubbish bags and tipped them out, strewing

garbage all over the neatly swept floor.

"Hey!" shouted Shelley. "We just tidied up."

Hex picked up the sleigh – and threw it through a window.

SMASH! The sleigh crashed through the window, scattering shards of glass over the floor. Then Hex picked up a metal bin and flung it through the next pane of glass.

"Stop that!" cried Kat. She darted towards Hex, but Mia and Charlotte pulled her back from the glass.

"Be careful," said Charlotte. "The glass is really sharp."

"You don't want to get cut," warned Mia.

Hex still wasn't done. He pulled an alarm and a siren started to blare.

PLIP! PLOP!

PLIP! PLOP!

Drops of water fell
on to Charlotte's head.
Looking up, she saw that
the alarm had set off the
emergency sprinklers in
the ceiling.

Charlotte ran over
to the alarm and tried
to switch it off but it
wouldn't budge. Hex
had jammed the lever.

WHEE-OOO!

WHEE-OOO!

"I can't turn it off!"

Charlotte shouted over the alarm's wails.

Mia ran over to help, but even using all their might, they couldn't pull the lever up. Water poured down from the sprinklers, soaking the girls. Puddles were beginning to form on the floor.

Covering their ears to block out the alarm's screeches, Kat and Shelley stared at the damage in horror.

"Now you won't get your wands," Hex taunted Mia and Charlotte. "Because the only thing anyone's getting right now is a detention!"

CHAPTER FIVE
Santa's Helpers

Miss Murphy, the headteacher, ran into the hall. "Where's the fire?" she yelled.

"It's a false alarm," said Shelley, shouting to be heard. "But we can't turn it off."

Miss Murphy waded through the puddles of water to a control panel on the wall. She keyed in a code and the alarm finally turned off. The sprinklers stopped too.

For a moment, Charlotte felt relieved, her ears still ringing from the alarm's screeches. But then she saw the stern look on the headteacher's face …

"What happened in here?" Miss Murphy asked, looking around at the broken windows,

puddles of water and garbage on the floor. "It looks like your bake sale got out of hand."

"It wasn't their fault," said Charlotte, pushing wet hair out of her face. She looked around for Hex, but Princess Poison's assistant had slipped out of the fire exit.

"The prom will have to be cancelled," said Miss Murphy, shaking her head. "There's no way we can hold an event in here. The money you've raised will have to pay for the damage."

Kat and Shelley looked stricken.

"We've got to do something," whispered Mia. "If the prom doesn't go ahead, we won't be able to grant their wishes."

Mia and Charlotte joined up their pendants. "I wish to fix the hall," whispered Charlotte.

A golden flash lit up the school hall. A moment later, the flooded floor was dry and the cracked windows were repaired. All of

the rubbish had been thrown away. The hall looked neat and tidy once more.

"It looks like the bake sale was a success, girls," said the headteacher. Like the rest of them, Miss Murphy was no longer soaking wet. "Well done." She looked around the hall approvingly. "Thanks for cleaning up."

"So we can still have the prom in here?" Kat asked nervously.

"Of course!" said Miss Murphy. The headteacher smiled at the girls. "Now I'm going home – to try a piece of my Christmas cake."

As soon as Miss Murphy had left the hall, Kat asked, "Why didn't she say anything about what just happened?"

"Yeah," said Shelley. "It was like she didn't even notice."

"She *didn't* notice," said Mia. "That's how the magic works."

"Only the people we're trying to help notice what's going on," said Charlotte.

The girls left school with Kat and Shelley and headed to the shopping centre. As they walked along, Charlotte asked, "What made you decide to have a prom?"

"We've seen them in movies," said Shelley. "And they look like fun. So we asked Miss Murphy if we could organise one."

"It's a chance to start a new winter tradition at our school," said Kat. "To make Christmastime even more special."

"I really wish we can raise a lot of money today," said Shelley. "To make sure our prom is as glamorous as the ones in films."

Charlotte glanced over at Mia. She knew exactly what her best friend was thinking – that they really needed to grant Shelley's wish. It wasn't just the prom that was at stake. Getting the candle relit would guarantee a happy Christmas for everyone!

As they walked through the shopping centre,

the girls stopped in front of a clothes shop.
They peered at a display of trendy party dresses
in the window.

"Ooh! I love that one!" squealed Kat,
pointing to a pretty pink dress with a layered
skirt and a sparkly belt.

"The lilac one's my favourite," said Shelley. The pale purple dress had a satin bodice and silver beads on the skirt.

"Come on," said Kat, tugging Shelley away from the window. "We've got work to do!"

In the middle of the shopping centre was a Santa's grotto. Behind a white picket fence there was a little wooden cottage surrounded by plastic reindeer and elves. A line of children were queueing to go inside and tell Santa their Christmas wishes.

Outside of the grotto, a table was set out with colourful wrapping paper, tape and ribbons. Shelley pulled a roll of card out of her bag. She unrolled it to reveal a sign that read: GIFT WRAPPING – SUPPORT OUR

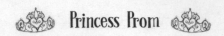

SCHOOL'S JINGLEBELL PROM.

Kat taped the sign to the front of the table. Then she took a big jar out of her schoolbag and put it on the table. The jar's label said: *Donations for the Prom.*

The gift-wrapping table quickly attracted a crowd of shoppers, all eager to have the presents they'd purchased wrapped. Mia wrapped a toy train set in paper decorated with shiny snowflakes.

"Here you go," said Kat, handing Mia a piece of tape.

"Oh, this is wonderful," said the old lady who'd bought it. "I've got arthritis and this saves me from having to wrap my grandson's gift." She dropped several coins into the jar.

Charlotte wrapped a fancy bottle of perfume in gold paper for a businessman wearing a smart grey suit. Then Shelley tied a red ribbon around the box.

"Thanks," the businessman said, as Shelley handed him the gift. "It looks great." He put money in the donations jar.

Charlotte could hear children in the queue to see Santa talking about what they wanted for Christmas. "Hey, Mia," she asked as she wrapped up a fluffy dressing gown, "what do you want for Christmas?"

Mia thought for a moment. "The only thing I really want is to become a Secret Princess," she said.

"Same here," said Charlotte. "It will be so

cool to get our wands. I can't wait."

"So let's make sure we grant Shelley and Kat's wishes!" said Mia, sticking a big gold bow on the jigsaw puzzle she had just wrapped.

"That's not going to happen," said the person standing at the front of the line.

Charlotte looked up and her heart sank. Princess Poison smirked down at her. Hex was at her side, his eyes narrowed and his arms crossed over his chest.

"I've got something for you girls," said Princess Poison. "But it's not a gift to wrap. It's something you'll never have – a wand!"

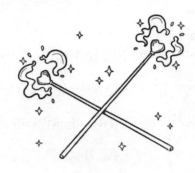

CHAPTER SIX
All Wrapped Up

Aiming her wand at the gift-wrapping station, Princess Poison narrowed her eyes and hissed out a spell:

Someone's wish is about to come undone,
Because causing trouble is much more fun!

Green light spewed out of the wand and

suddenly Charlotte realised she couldn't move. Looking down, she saw that Princess Poison's magic had wound sticky tape all around her, pinning her arms to her sides. The spell had turned Mia and Charlotte into mummies! And that wasn't the worst of it – all the presents that the girls had carefully wrapped were ripped and torn, the boxes crushed and dented.

"I can see that you're a bit *tied* up," said Princess Poison. "We're off to do some shopping."

As the baddies sauntered off, the shoppers examined their ruined presents.

"They broke my perfume bottle," said the businessman. The box Charlotte had wrapped was squashed, the gold paper soggy. A strong flowery scent wafted from the box.

"My grandson's train set is ruined," wailed the old woman. She shook the badly dented box and pieces rattled around inside. "And it was the last one in the shop."

As angry shoppers complained about their ruined presents, Charlotte hopped over to Mia. "We've got to sort this out," she said.

"Can you give us a hand?" Mia called.

Kat and Shelley held Mia and Charlotte's pendants together. Because there was only enough magic left to make one more wish, the heart glowed very faintly.

"I wish for all the presents to be beautifully wrapped," said Mia.

The last of the magic shot out of the heart, setting Mia and Charlotte free from their sticky-tape bindings. The broken gifts were now repaired and wrapped in shiny paper, with curly ribbons and silky bows.

"Well, that was a sticky situation," joked Charlotte. But deep down she knew that it was no laughing matter – now they didn't have any wishes left to help them stop Princess Poison.

The girls returned to wrapping presents.
They sang Christmas carols as they worked
and people waiting in the queue joined in.

"What do elves learn at school?" Charlotte
asked a little girl who'd bought a coffee mug
for her dad.

"How to wrap gifts?" guessed the little girl.

"No," said Charlotte. "The elf-abet!"

The little girl chuckled, then told Charlotte a joke about a snowman. Soon everyone in the queue was sharing Christmas jokes. The donations jar got fuller and fuller as the girls wrapped present after present.

"Coming through!" called Hex, shoving the other shoppers aside. He and Princess Poison barged their way to the front of the queue.

"I've been buying presents – for myself, of course," Princess Poison said, dropping several shopping bags on the table.

"What do you think you're doing?" Charlotte demanded. "You can't just cut ahead of everyone their turn."

"I'm jumping the queue," said Princess

Poison, her eyes glinting maliciously. "Nothing's more likely to get stressed-out Christmas shoppers angry." "They'll get so annoyed they'll leave," said Hex gleefully. "And then you won't raise any more money for the prom."

Charlotte glanced nervously at the queue of shoppers patiently waiting to have their gifts wrapped. Instead of looking cross, they were happily trading jokes and chatting to each other. Princess Poison's plan didn't seem to be working …

"What's wrong with these people?" Princess Poison hissed, scowling. "Why aren't they getting upset?"

"Because they have something that you don't have," said Mia. "Christmas spirit."

"Christmas is a time to be nice to other people," said Charlotte. "You two might want to try it."

Mia and Charlotte began singing *We Wish You a Merry Christmas* and the people in the queue joined in, their voices swelling to fill the shopping centre with music.

"Aaargghh!" shrieked Princess Poison, covering her ears. "I can't stand all this merriness. I've got to get out of here!"

Hex grabbed the shopping bags and hurried after Princess Poison as she stormed off.

"Sorry about that," Charlotte apologised to the people waiting in the queue.

"No problem," said a man holding a shopping bag from a toy store. "We're having so much fun we don't mind waiting."

The girls continued wrapping presents. Soon the donations jar was so full there wasn't room for another penny. When there were no more people waiting, Kat and Shelley counted the donations as Mia and Charlotte tidied away the wrapping paper.

"We did it!" exclaimed Shelley, beaming. "We made enough money today to pay for the prom – and there's lots left over!"

"We're going to give the extra money to charity!" said Kat. "To help needy families."

"That's a lovely idea," said Mia.

Shelley nodded. "Not everyone is as lucky as we are at Christmastime."

A soft jingling noise came from Santa's grotto. Charlotte turned and saw that the two plastic reindeer had been replaced with real reindeer! Bells around their necks jingled as children stroked their soft fur.

"Is that Joy and Noelle?" said Mia.

"It certainly looks like them," said Charlotte.

"Did you two make the reindeer appear?" Shelley asked, her eyes wide.

"Not exactly," said Mia. "Our princess friends sent them because we granted your wish."

"That's not the only thing that's appeared," said Kat, pointing at the girls' feet. The girls' shoes had been replaced with their sparkling ruby slippers.

"That means we need to go home now," said Charlotte.

"Thank you so much for helping us out today," said Shelley, pulling the girls into a group hug. "We couldn't have raised all that money for the prom without you."

"Hopefully it will be a really amazing night," said Kat.

"Will you come back for it?" asked Shelley. "It's on the fifteenth of December."

"I hope so," said Mia, "because we've still got to grant Kat's wish of making the Jinglebell Prom a success."

"See you on prom night, Mia," said Charlotte, squeezing her best friend's hand.

Mia and Charlotte clicked the heels of their ruby slippers together three times. "Home!" they both cried, waving goodbye to their new friends.

The magic took Charlotte back to the school Christmas fair. No time had passed there while she was gone. Charlotte suddenly knew exactly what to get Mia for Christmas. She went back to the stall selling ornaments and bought one

shaped like a unicorn. It was white and had
a pearly horn – just like Angel, Snowy and
Frosty. Charlotte knew it would remind Mia of
their unicorn ride at Wishing Star Palace.

Hopefully, the next time they visited the
palace something even more amazing would
happen. If they granted one more wish, they'd

earn their wands! Charlotte grinned and
hugged herself with excitement. If she and Mia
became Secret Princesses, it would be the best
Christmas ever!

Story Two

CHAPTER ONE

Princess Portraits

Mia was decorating the Christmas tree with her mum and her little sister, Elsie. Mum finished winding fairy lights around the branches and switched them on.

"Ta da!" Mum announced.

"Ooh! Pretty!" said Elsie, clapping her hands as the colourful lights twinkled.

Mum opened up a big box of ornaments.

"You made this one when you were in nursery, Mia," said Mum, holding up an angel made from a wooden clothes peg. It had yellow wool for hair.

"I'm a bit better at crafts now," said Mia, grinning. She took out a little Santa Claus she'd knitted last year and hung it on the tree.

"Can I put the star on the top, Mummy?" asked Elsie.

"Of course," said Mum. She picked Elsie up. Elsie stretched out her chubby arms and put the star on the top of the tree.

Seeing the star made Mia think of Wishing Star Palace. Today was the fifteenth of December – the day of the Jinglebell Prom! All day long, she'd been checking her necklace

anxiously to see if the pendant was glowing.

DING DONG!

Mum put Elsie down and went to answer the front door.

"It's for you, Mia," said Mum, handing Mia a parcel.

"It's from Charlotte!" Mia said as she spotted the American stamps and her best friend's loopy handwriting.

Mia opened the box and unwrapped the unicorn ornament.

"Oh!" she gasped. "It's beautiful!"

Mia hung the unicorn on the Christmas

tree. Its pearly horn shimmered in the fairy lights' colourful glow.

"What a thoughtful gift," said Mum. "Charlotte obviously remembers how much you love animals."

Mia smiled and nodded. Of course she couldn't tell Mum that Charlotte had chosen the ornament to remind her of the incredible unicorn ride they'd shared on their last visit to Wishing Star Palace!

Glancing down at her necklace again, Mia nearly let out a shout of joy. Her pendant was glowing at last!

"I'm going to send Charlotte an email to say thank you," she said, hurrying out of the room.

Going into her bedroom, Mia shut the door

and grasped the pendant, her hands trembling with excitement.

"I wish I could see Charlotte," Mia said.

Magical light from the pendant whisked Mia to Wishing Star Palace. Charlotte was waiting for her by the Christmas tree, wearing her pink princess dress.

"Thank you so much for my unicorn," said Mia, bounding over to hug her friend. "It arrived

just before my necklace started glowing."

"I've been checking my necklace all day long," said Charlotte.

"Me too!" said Mia.

A dark-haired princess in a yellow dress bustled into the entrance hall, holding a poinsettia with red flowers and a spray of mistletoe. Princess Evie, whose pendant was shaped like a flower, had a special talent for gardening.

"Hi, Evie," said Mia. "How are you?"

"Busy," said Evie. "We've all been granting Christmas wishes. We've made almost enough magic to relight the candle again."

"That's awesome," said Mia.

"That's why we're here," said Charlotte.

"To grant our second Christmas wish."

"First you need to open a door in the advent calendar," said Evie, ushering them into the sitting room. She placed the poinsettia on a side table and hung the sprig of mistletoe above the doorway.

The Secret Princesses were all getting into the Christmas spirit! Princess Cara, a fashion designer, was embroidering Princess Ella's name on a silk Christmas stocking. Princess Sylvie was passing around a plate of gingerbread princesses and Princess Alice was strumming Christmas songs on her guitar.

"That's a pretty stocking," Mia told Cara.

"Thanks," said Cara. "I made one for every princess. You and Charlotte, too."

She rummaged in the sewing basket at her feet, then pulled out a pink stocking with Charlotte's name on it and a gold stocking with Mia's name on it.

"They match our dresses," said Charlotte.

"But we're not Secret Princesses yet," Mia reminded Cara.

"You will be soon," said Alice, coming over and kissing both girls on the cheek.

"Now that Mia and Charlotte are here, I want to take a photo," said Princess Kiko, arranging everyone in front of the advent calendar. "Everyone smile!" said the gymnast princess, pressing a button on her camera. Kiko did a handspring across the room and got into the shot just before the flash went off.

"Come on," Evie urged Mia. "Open a door."

Mia searched for the number fifteen. Several windows and doors had been opened since their last visit. She found a window marked *fifteen* at the top of the palace's astronomy tower.

Mia opened the window and a rainbow beamed out, stretching across the room. The

words written on the back of the window said,
A picture painted by Princess Sophie.

Sophie clapped her hands. "Yay! Let's get started straight away!"

She sat Mia on a comfy footstool in front of the fire and started drawing.

"Wait!" said Mia. "Charlotte shared her gift with me. Can she be in the painting too?"

"Good idea," said Sophie. "I need to do a painting of the two of you for the Portrait Gallery, so this can be it."

"But we're not Secret Princesses yet," Mia said again as Charlotte squeezed in next to her. She didn't want to take anything for granted.

"You will be soon," murmured Princess Sophie, busily sketching.

"Not according to Princess Poison," said Mia.

"Well, it's a good thing we never believe anything Princess Poison says," said Charlotte.

The Secret Princesses' wands suddenly started to flash.

"Is it time to grant Kat's wish?" asked Mia.

Princess Alice nodded. "Have fun at the Jinglebell Prom!"

Mia and Charlotte raced back to the Christmas tree in the entrance hall. Shelley and Kat's faces had appeared in the baubles.

"Let's do this!" said Charlotte, sounding determined.

The girls each held a bauble.

"Shelley!" cried Charlotte.

"Kat!" exclaimed Mia.

The magic swept them away from the palace. They were off to grant another wish – the most important one ever!

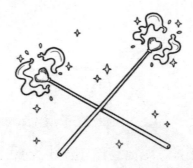

CHAPTER TWO
Prom Pampering

The magic set the girls down in a bedroom with peach-coloured walls, a single bed and a dressing table. Two pairs of startled eyes stared out at them from green faces.

"Er, hello?" said Mia, wondering whether they'd come to the wrong place – or even the wrong planet!

"You came!" cried one of the green-faced

girls, jumping off the bed. She was wearing a
dressing gown and her hair was wrapped in a
towel like a turban. "We're still getting ready!"

Mia laughed, recognising Kat's voice. "I
didn't realise it was you for a second. You look
like aliens."

"We made face masks as part of our pre-prom
pampering," explained Shelley.

"Do you want one too?" asked Kat.

"Yes, please!" said Charlotte.

"What's in this?" asked Charlotte as Shelley slathered her face with bright green goop. "It smells good."

"It's got mashed-up avocado, yoghurt and honey," said Shelley.

"I found the recipe in a magazine," said Kat, spreading the mixture on Mia's face. "It's supposed to make your skin feel nice."

"It tastes nice too," said Mia, licking a tiny bit off the corner of her mouth.

As they waited for their face masks to dry, Kat put on a pop music playlist on her phone.

"So have you two been busy since we last saw you?" Charlotte asked.

Shelley nodded. "We had so much stuff to sort out – the DJ, the food and the decorations."

"But it's going to be totally worth it," said Kat. "All the tickets sold out and everyone's really excited about tonight."

"That's great," said Mia.

"I really wish that it will all go well," said Kat nervously.

"That's why we're here," Charlotte reminded her. "To grant your wish."

Kat grinned at them. "Now that you two are here, it's sure to be a magical night!"

Mia and Charlotte exchanged looks. They both desperately hoped that the only magic tonight would be good magic. If Princess

Poison ruined the prom, she'd spoil their chances of becoming Secret Princesses!

The girls rinsed the green goop off their faces, leaving their skin soft and smooth. Alice's latest Christmas song, called *The Greatest Gift*, started to play as Mia painted sparkly polish on to Kat's fingernails.

"Ooh! I love Alice de Silver!" squealed Kat, singing along.

"So do we," said Mia, sharing a secret smile with Charlotte.

As she finished doing Kat's nails, Mia thought about how much she wanted to make Alice proud. After all, Alice had given them the greatest gift of all – the chance to become Secret Princesses!

When everyone's nails were dry, Mia and
Charlotte helped style Kat and Shelley's hair.
Mia plaited Kat's brown hair around her head
like a crown. Charlotte put a little jewelled
tiara on Shelley's blonde bob.

"What are you wearing tonight?" Mia asked.

"We'll show you," replied Kat. The girls changed into the prom dresses they'd seen at the shopping centre.

Kat looked amazing in a pink dress with a soft, floaty skirt. Shelley was wearing a sparkly lilac-coloured dress tied with a big, silky bow at the back.

"I feel like a princess," said Kat. She and Shelley stood in front of the mirror on the front of her wardrobe.

"You look like one too," said Mia.

Suddenly, the image in the mirror changed. "There's only one princess here," said Princess Poison. "And that's me."

Kat and Shelley shrank back in fear as Princess Poison stepped right out of the mirror.

"You SHAN'T go to the ball," said Princess Poison.

She brandished her wand at Kat and Shelley and spat out a spell:

Shred their dresses into tattered rags.
Turn these prom queens into hags!

Green light flew out of Princess Poison's wand and landed on Kat and Shelley. Their pretty pastel prom dresses were now shapeless sacks made of dirty brown and grey rags. The girls looked as though they'd been rolling in dirt instead of pampering themselves!

"I hope there's something good on television tonight," said Princess Poison, "Because you can't go to the prom looking like that." Then she stepped back into the mirror and disappeared.

"She's right," wailed Kat. "We're the organisers. We can't turn up at the prom in these rags."

"We've got this," said Charlotte. She held her glowing pendant against Mia's.

"I wish for beautiful prom dresses," said Mia.

Golden light from the heart transformed Kat and Shelley's clothes back into prom dresses. But they weren't the same outfits they'd had on before – now they were even more stunning!

Shelley wore an elegant violet silk frock and sparkly gold slippers. Kat's dress had a bright

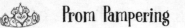

pink satin bodice and a ballerina-style skirt
made of pale pink chiffon. She had dainty
silver sandals on her feet.

"The magic gave you guys prom dresses too!"
cried Kat.

Mia and Charlotte ran to the mirror.

"Wow!" gasped Mia, staring at their

reflection. She had on a lacy powder-blue dress with a pleated skirt, while Charlotte looked lovely in a pale yellow dress with daisies on it and a pretty white cardigan.

"This is so cool!" said Charlotte, twirling in front of the mirror.

KNOCK! KNOCK!

"Are you girls ready?" called Kat's mum. "I'd like to take some pictures before you go."

"Coming!" said Kat, stuffing her phone into her bag.

Chatting excitedly, the girls trooped downstairs to Kat's living room. Thanks to the way the magic worked, Kat's parents didn't wonder why Mia and Charlotte were there.

"Don't you all look lovely," said Kat's dad.

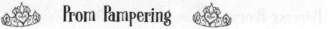

Kat's mum snapped dozens of photos.

BEEP BEEP!

"That must be the limo!" exclaimed Kat.

The girls ran to the window and drew back the curtain.

But it wasn't a big, black limousine parked outside the house – it was a big, smelly bin lorry! Leaning out of the window, the driver waved to them, a nasty smirk on his face.

It was Hex!

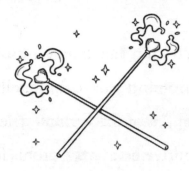

CHAPTER THREE
A Grand Entrance

"We can't turn up to the prom in a bin lorry!" wailed Kat.

"That would be really embarrassing," said Shelley, looking mortified.

"There must have been some mix-up with the booking," said Kat's dad.

Mia caught Charlotte's eye. They knew it wasn't a mistake. It was all part of Princess

Poison's plan to ruin Kat's wish – and stop them from becoming Secret Princesses!

"Don't worry," said Kat's mum, grabbing her car keys. "I'll drive you to the prom."

When they went outside, the bin lorry was still there but Hex had disappeared. The foul odour of rotten food and rubbish wafted over to them.

"Ugh!" said Shelley, holding her nose. "That truck stinks."

"How am I going to get out with that thing blocking the drive?" said Kat's mum, frowning.

"Oh no!" said Kat. "We're going to be so late! This is a disaster!"

"Don't worry," said Mia. "Charlotte and I will get you to the prom in time."

The girls held their
pendants together.

"I wish for the girls to
get to the prom in style,"
said Charlotte.

Dazzling light streamed
out of the heart, getting
rid of the rubbish truck.

*CLIP CLOP! CLIP
CLOP!*

"What's that noise?"
asked Kat.

"It sounds like hooves,"
said Mia.

A gold carriage pulled
by two white horses

trotted down the street and stopped in front
of Kat's house. The horses had white plumes
on their heads and bells on their harnesses.
Princess Ella, wearing a footman's uniform,
was holding the reins.

Ella winked at Mia and Charlotte. "Your
carriage awaits," she said grandly, hopping
down to open the carriage door.

"OMG!" exclaimed Kat. "This is like
something out of a fairy tale!"

Kat and Shelley climbed into the carriage,
then Mia and Charlotte settled into the seat
facing them. The girls snuggled together
on the plush red velvet seats, pulling furry
blankets around themselves to stay warm.

"Goodbye!" called Kat's mum. Snapping a

few more photos, she waved them off happily.

Ella gave a light flick of the reins and the
horses trotted off, the bells on their harnesses
jingling merrily. Just when Mia thought
the journey couldn't get any more magical,
snowflakes began to fall!

"Talk about making a big entrance," said Kat as the horses stopped in front of the school. All around them, boys and girls were getting out of limousines, wearing elegant dresses and smart suits. But nobody else had arrived in a horse-drawn carriage!

The girls stepped down from the carriage, on to the red carpet.

"Thanks, guys," said Mia, patting both of the horses.

"Have fun tonight," said Ella. Then, lowering her voice to a whisper, she added, "And good luck!"

The four girls walked down the red carpet, arm in arm. Inside the school, an archway of white and silver balloons led into the hall.

"Wow!" exclaimed Mia, when they got to the end. "You two did an amazing job decorating."

The hall looked like a winter wonderland! Shimmering swags of white silk draped the ceiling. Silver snowflakes seemed to float in mid-air. A blanket of fake snow covered the floor. White fairy lights twinkled on every wall and ice sculptures shaped like angels stood in each corner of the room. The tables were set with crisp white tablecloths, with centrepieces of white and red roses on each one.

Kat and Shelley led the girls to a big Christmas tree decorated with white lights and silver baubles. Underneath it were piles of beautifully wrapped presents.

"Who are these for?" asked Charlotte.

"For families in need," explained Shelley. "We bought toys and clothes with the extra money we raised. We're going to deliver the presents to a local charity just before Christmas Eve."

As Kat and Shelley posed for selfies and admired their classmates' outfits, Mia and Charlotte gazed at the presents under the tree.

"I love it when our wishes help lots of people," said Mia.

"Kat and Shelley are amazing," said Charlotte. "Let's tell the others about them back at the palace. They might have what it takes to become Secret Princesses."

"Hopefully there will be a vacancy for two new trainees soon," said Mia, grinning.

Charlotte grinned back at Mia, but her smile quickly faded into a frown.

"What's wrong?" asked Mia.

"I'll give you two clues," said Charlotte. "Her initials are P.P. and she isn't here to enjoy the party ..."

Mia turned and saw Princess Poison sweep through the archway of balloons in a long green ballgown.

"You shouldn't be here," said Charlotte, marching over to her. "You don't have a ticket for the prom."

"Enjoy being prom princesses," mocked Princess Poison. "Because that's the only type of princess you'll ever be."

Charlotte held her thumb and index finger a centimetre apart. "We're this close to becoming Secret Princesses," she told Princess Poison. "There's no way you're going to stop us."

"And when we do become Secret Princesses," Mia said, "we'll never be as foolish as you and throw it all away by being selfish."

"What good is magic if you can't use it to help yourself?" sneered Princess Poison. "The Secret Princesses are the fools – not me."

"No they aren't!" Mia retorted loyally. "Nothing feels better than using magic to help other people."

Princess Poison twiddled the poison bottle pendant on her necklace for a moment, a sly look stealing across her face. "OK," she said sweetly. "Just to prove that I do know about helping other people, I'm going to help the two of you."

Charlotte let out a snort of disbelief.

"Instead of signing up for a life of boring do-gooding, you can team up with me," said Princess Poison, tapping her wand against her hand. "You'd get your very own wands right away. Just think – you can use them to grant your own wishes and become much more powerful than any silly Secret Princess could ever be."

Mia and Charlotte stared at Princess Poison in stunned silence.

"So what do you say?" Princess Poison looked at them expectantly. "Yes or no?"

Mia and Charlotte didn't even need to consider her offer for a second.

"NO!" they shouted.

CHAPTER FOUR
Chocolate Flood

Princess Poison angrily jabbed a balloon with her long fingernail, popping it.

"You'll regret that!" she hissed, glowering at the girls.

"No, we won't," said Charlotte. "You made us that offer once before and we turned you down – and that was before we even knew how horrible you are."

A waiter came by, offering them glasses of creamy eggnog with a little candy cane stuck in each one. Princess Poison waved him away impatiently.

"You tiresome twerps!" she shrieked at the girls, her green eyes flashing with fury. "You annoying little goody-goodies. You—"

CLINK! CLINK! CLINK!

Kat tapped a spoon against her glass of eggnog to get everyone's attention, cutting off Princess Poison's insults. The prom guests, who were chatting in small groups, stopped talking and listened. Princess Poison gave a loud huff and stormed across the hall, pulling out a phone as she went.

"Thank you all for coming," Kat told to the

prom-goers. "And for supporting our fundraisers these past few weeks."

"We raised more than we needed for the prom, so we've used the extra money to buy presents for families in need this Christmas," announced Shelley.

The prom guests applauded.

"We hope you all have a great night," said Kat. "The buffet is now open!"

Hungry boys and girls rushed towards the buffet. The food looked delicious. There were stuffed mushrooms, tiny cheese tarts, prawns on little skewers, cocktail sausages and delicate puff pastries.

"Aren't you going to eat?" Charlotte asked Mia, holding a plate of food.

"My tummy's in knots," Mia said, shaking her head. She glanced over to the corner where Princess Poison was talking into her phone, a furious look on her face. "I've never seen her so angry before. I'm sure she's going to try something really terrible."

Charlotte shrugged. "Whatever she throws at us, we can take it."

Mia glanced down at her necklace anxiously. Her pendant was glowing very faintly. "We only have enough magic left to make one more wish."

"Magic or no magic," said Charlotte, "NOTHING is going to stop us from granting Kat's wish and making this prom lots of fun." She popped a mushroom in her mouth.

Her best friend's cheerful determination made Mia feel better. She helped herself to some food.

"Yum," she said, sampling a cheese tart. "These are really good."

The girls went over to Shelley and Kat's table. The prom organisers were whispering to each other.

"Is everything OK?" asked Mia, sitting down next to them.

"It's the DJ we booked," said Shelley, biting her lip nervously. "He hasn't turned up yet."

"It's probably because of the snow," said Charlotte reassuringly.

"I hope you're right," said Kat. "Because everyone is expecting awesome dance music."

Mia darted a look at Princess Poison. She had stopped talking on the phone and was nibbling a prawn skewer from the buffet. *Uh-oh*, thought Mia. Princess Poison looked worryingly pleased with herself ...

For dessert, there was a chocolate fountain with fruit, marshmallows and biscuits to dip in the melted chocolate. There was also a candy buffet with jars of sweets – from jellybeans and fizzy cola bottles to strawberry bonbons and liquorice allsorts.

Mia dipped a strawberry into chocolate.

"What kind of bear has no teeth?" Charlotte asked her friends as she helped herself to some sweeties.

Mia couldn't reply – her mouth was too full of chocolate and strawberry!

"A gummy bear!" said Charlotte, holding up a sweet.

Mia groaned, but she couldn't help smiling. No matter how cheesy Charlotte's jokes were, they always cheered her up.

"Aww," said Princess Poison, sidling up to them. "You two are just so sweet. I just love sweet things." She pointed her wand at the chocolate fountain.

Green light hit the chocolate, making it bubble. Chocolate spewed out, spilling over

the sides of the fountain
and pouring on to the floor.
Soon the snowy white dance
floor was covered with a
melted chocolate mudslide!

"Oh no!" cried Kat as
chocolate pooled around her
ankles, ruining her sparkly
silver shoes. "What a mess!"

Princess Poison pouted. "I was just trying to help," she said. "I thought everyone liked sweet things." Giving Mia and Charlotte an arch look, she strutted away, lifting her long skirts to avoid the chocolate.

"What are we going to do?" worried Shelley. "We can't dance with chocolate on the floor."

"Cool!" shouted a boy in a tuxedo. He ran and slid across the chocolate-covered floor, sinking to his knees like a football player celebrating a goal.

A girl in a pale green prom dress copied him, taking off her high heels and sliding across the floor. "Whee!" she shouted.

Soon, all of the prom guests were slipping and sliding in the chocolate. Even Miss

Murphy, who was chaperoning the prom, had a go! Everyone's fancy clothes got covered in chocolate, but they were all having so much fun they didn't care!

As she held hands with Charlotte and slid across the floor, Mia saw Princess Poison glaring at them. She had been trying to cause trouble, but her plan had backfired.

The chocolate mudslide was a hit!

RING! RING!

Kat answered her phone, then smiled with relief.

"That was the DJ," she told the others. "He'll be here soon."

"We'd better clean this up then," said Mia.

She and Charlotte held their pendants together and used their last wish to clean up the chocolate. The floor – and everyone's outfits – were spotless once more.

Moments later, a short, tubby man in a shiny green tracksuit swaggered into the hall. He wore sunglasses, a baseball cap turned backwards and loads of thick, gold chains. He was dressed like a rap star, but Mia would have recognised Hex anywhere from the smug smirk on his face.

"Yo!" said Hex. "DJ Hex is here to get this party started."

"You're not the DJ we booked," said Kat, looking confused.

"About that," said Princess Poison, coming over to them. "I rang the DJ and told him the prom was cancelled because of the snow. So DJ Hex stepped in to save the day."

"Word!" said Hex,

crossing his arms over his burly chest.

Kat and Shelley stared at him in dismay.

Hex swaggered over to the DJ booth and started fiddling with the equipment.

"We promised people there would be a good DJ," said Kat.

"Maybe he'll be OK," said Shelley hopefully, as Hex twirled a record around on his fingertip.

"Whazzup!" Hex said into the microphone. "Are you ready to party?"

The prom guests whooped and rushed on to the dance floor. Special disco lights projected snowflake patterns on the ceiling and the dance floor.

Hex put a record on. The shrill sound of pan pipes filled the air. The students looked at each other in confusion. A few tried to dance, but quickly gave up.

"This is rubbish," someone shouted.

A horrible scratching sound pierced the air as Hex changed the record. Wincing, the prom guests covered their ears.

DJ Hex's next choice was no better. It sounded like whales calling to each other underwater.

"Play something we can dance to!" shouted a girl in a red dress.

Ignoring her, DJ Hex threw his arms in the air and shouted, "Come on, party people! Show me your moves!"

A slow, mournful song, with lots of wailing bagpipes, began to play.

Shaking their heads, boys and girls walked off the dance floor in disgust. The only person dancing was Princess Poison, who was spinning and waving her arms in the air wildly.

"Can you do some magic?" begged Kat. "And wish for a new DJ?"

"I'm sorry," said Charlotte. "We only have

enough magic to grant three small wishes –
and we've used all of them all up."

Kat's face fell. "So my wish isn't going to be
granted now?"

Princess Poison danced up to them. "That's right," she gloated. "Unlike your little friends here, my power is unlimited." Scowling at Mia and Charlotte, she added, "Yours would be too if you'd made the right choice."

A group of prom guests walked past, grumbling about the DJ.

"Face it," said Princess Poison. "The Jinglebell Prom is ruined!"

A tear trickled down Kat's cheek. Shelley comforted her friend, but Mia could see that she was on the verge of tears too. The girls had worked so hard to make the prom a success – they couldn't let Princess Poison spoil it!

"Not so fast," said Mia. "You don't need a DJ to have a good party."

"That's right," said Charlotte. "You just need something you don't have, Princess Poison – FRIENDS!"

CHAPTER FIVE
The Greatest Gift

Mia turned to Kat and said, "Please can I borrow your phone?"

Kat rummaged in her bag and handed Mia her phone.

Mia ran to the DJ booth and plugged Kat's phone into the sound system. She found the playlist they'd been listening to while they were getting ready and turned it on. A catchy

pop song started to blast out of the speakers.

"Come on, everyone!" called Charlotte, twirling around. "Party time!"

"This is more like it!" said a boy in a tuxedo, running on to the dance floor.

Soon, every prom guest was dancing with their friends. Mia and Charlotte joined in with the fun. They spun around the dance floor, their prom dresses swirling around their legs as they moved to the beat.

"Do something, Hex!" snarled Princess Poison.

But before Hex could respond, Miss Murphy dragged him on to the dance floor. The headteacher had let her hair down from its usual tight bun and she was wearing a prettty,

flowery dress. Smiling, she and Hex jived to a fast-paced pop song.

"Look at Hex!" giggled Charlotte.

"He's not a bad dancer," said Mia.

"Way to go, Miss Murphy!" called Shelley.

"Everyone's having fun," said Kat, beaming. "The prom is a success. You granted my wish after all!"

Just then, Alice's new Christmas song began to play. But the sound wasn't coming from Kat's phone – Alice was at the prom, singing live!

"SQUEE!" shrieked Shelley and Kat. "It's Alice de Silver!"

Alice belted out *The Greatest Gift*. As the

prom guests went wild, magical snowflakes
fluttered down from the ceiling. Everyone
linked arms and swayed in the snow, singing
along to Alice's song. Kat's wish had been
granted!

"We're going!" Princess Poison hissed at Hex,
grabbing his arm.

"No," said Hex, shaking his head. "I'm
having too much fun. I'm tired of the way you
treat me." He danced off with Miss Murphy in
his arms.

Stamping her foot, Princess Poison let out a
shriek of frustration. Mia almost felt sorry for
her. Hex was the closest thing Princess Poison
had to a friend.

Her sympathy soon evaporated as Princess

Poison snapped at her. "What are you looking at? This isn't over." She waved her wand and vanished in a flash of green light.

Alice finished her song to cheers and thunderous applause.

"Thank you," said Alice, smiling at the crowd. "I'm dedicating my next song to two very special friends. When they work together, they can do anything they set their minds to."

Alice launched into her hit single, *Best Friends*.

Mia turned to Charlotte, an enormous grin on her face.

"We did it!" said Charlotte, her eyes shining. "We granted a double wish!"

"Thank you so much," said Shelley, coming

over with Kat. "This is incredible. I don't know how you managed to get Alice de Silver here."

"You guys are amazing," said Kat, nodding.

"It's because we granted your wish," explained Charlotte.

Listening to Alice sing about friendship, Mia looked at the piles of presents under the Christmas tree.

"You two are amazing, too," Mia told Kat and Shelley. "Tonight was fun, but it also helped a lot of people. All because you two worked together."

Alice finished her song and came to find Mia and Charlotte. "We've got to go now," she told Shelley and Kat.

The girls hugged Mia and Charlotte

goodbye, then Alice waved her wand. Magic instantly carried them back to the palace.

Above the fireplace, the Christmas Candle shone brightly, its flame filling the entrance hall with magical light and making the diamonds in the girls' tiaras twinkle.

"Because of the Christmas wish you just granted, we finally had enough magic to be able to relight the candle," said Alice. "Now everyone will have a merry Christmas."

She led the girls to the ballroom and threw open the doors. Mia and Charlotte gasped. The Secret Princesses stood facing each other in two lines, holding their wands across the gap to make a glowing archway.

Holding hands, Mia and Charlotte walked

through the archway. Their princess friends beamed at them, murmuring congratulations. At the end of the archway, Princess Anna was waiting for them by two gold thrones.

"Congratulations on completing your final task, my dears," said the wise princess. "It is

time to make your Secret Princess promise."

Sitting on the thrones, Mia and Charlotte faced their princess friends and recited:

I promise that I will be kind and brave,
Using my magic to help and save.
Granting wishes and doing my best,
To make people smile and bring happiness.

When they were finished, Princess Anna said, "As you are Friendship Princesses, you must solemnly swear to remain best friends for ever."

Looking deep into her best friend's eyes, Mia pressed her pendant against Charlotte's.

"Best friends for ever!" they exclaimed.

Heart-shaped sparkles flew out of the gold heart and showered down over the ballroom. The bells in Wishing Star Palace's towers chimed joyously as the Secret Princesses clapped and cheered. Mia squeezed Charlotte's hand, too full of emotion to speak.

Alice came forward, holding two gold wands with hearts on their tips. "I always knew your friendship was special," she said, beaming.

"I'm so proud of you both." She handed them each a wand.

"Now raise your wands …" Princess Anna instructed the other Secret Princesses.

The Secret Princesses lifted their wands and pointed them at Mia and Charlotte.

"… and share your magic with Princess Mia and Princess Charlotte!"

Magical light streamed out of every princess's wand, filling Mia and Charlotte's wands with magic. Mia felt herself glowing with love and happiness, as the Secret Princesses bestowed their powers upon her and Charlotte.

"Hurrah!" cheered the princesses, throwing their wands into the air in celebration.

BANG!

The doors burst open and someone stormed into the ballroom. The Secret Princesses let out a collective gasp.

Princess Poison was at the palace!

CHAPTER SIX
Princess Power

"How did you get in here?" asked Princess Anna.

"It was simple," gloated Princess Poison. "You're forgetting that I used to be one of you. I knew that all the magic at Wishing Star Palace would be focussed on those two pests during the princess ceremony. In that moment, all the usual spells protecting the palace were

lifted." She smirked. "And a moment was all I needed to get inside."

"You need to leave," said Princess Alice, confronting Princess Poison. "You were banished long ago."

"Oh, but I've missed it here," said Princess Poison, flopping down on one of the gold thrones. "So don't think you're going to get

rid of me again." She crossed her legs and gazed around the ballroom dismissively. "I see not much has changed. Time to do some redecorating." She waved her wand and the walls and curtains changed to an ugly shade of green.

"Stop that!" shouted Charlotte. "The only thing wrong with the palace is that you're here!"

"Wishing Star Palace belongs to me now," snapped Princess Poison. "So I can do whatever I please."

"No, it doesn't!" yelled Mia. "It belongs to the Secret Princesses – and you don't deserve to be one."

Princess Poison stood up, her eyes narrowing.

"You think you're so special now that you have your magic wands," spat Princess Poison. "Well, that's another thing I'm going to change."

She pointed her wand at Mia and Charlotte.

Take their wands and magic powers,
Never to return to the palace's towers!

Green magic blasted out of Princess Poison's wand, flying towards the girls.

Quick as a flash, Mia's instincts took over. She couldn't let Princess Poison take away her best friend's powers. Not after they had worked so hard to pass their training and all they had been through together.

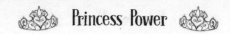

"Keep Charlotte safe!" she cried, aiming her wand at Charlotte.

At the very same moment, Charlotte pointed her wand at Mia, calling out, "Protect Mia!"

Glittering golden light shot out of both wands. The good magic hovered in the air in front of Mia and Charlotte, protecting each of them like a shield.

Princess Poison's spell hit the golden shield and rebounded – flying back to hit her instead!

"NOOOOO!" Princess Poison screeched, staring at her empty hand in horror. The wand she had been pointing at them a second ago had vanished.

Clutching her poison bottle necklace, she screamed, "I wish for the Secret Princesses to lose their magic!"

Nothing happened. Princess Poison's magic necklace wasn't working either!

"THIS CAN'T BE HAPPENING!" shrieked

Princess Poison,
sinking to
her knees and
pounding the floor
with her fists.

"I'm afraid it is,"
said Mia gently,
feeling a pang of
pity. Without her
magic, Princess
Poison had nothing. Even if her spell had
worked and stripped away Mia and Charlotte's
wands and magic, the best friends would have
still had each other. Princess Poison didn't
even have Hex any more.

"You knew that Secret Princesses wouldn't

use their magic to save themselves," said Charlotte. "But you forgot that Friendship Princesses always look out for each other."

"It's time for you to leave," Alice told Princess Poison. "Never come here again." She waved her wand and Princess Poison vanished.

"Yay!" cheered Charlotte, punching the air. "Princess Poison is gone! She'll never cause trouble for the Secret Princesses again!"

"I wouldn't be so sure about that," said Alice. "Knowing Princess Poison, she'll find a way."

"Maybe she'll change," said Mia. "Perhaps she's finally learned that friendship is more powerful than magic."

"I hope you're right," said Alice, ruffling Mia's hair affectionately.

"Now let's celebrate!" called Princess Sylvie.

"Can we test out our wands?" asked Charlotte eagerly.

"I think you already have," chuckled Sylvie.

Mia waved her wand, getting rid of the horrible green walls and curtains. Now, the ballroom sparkled with fairy lights. Garlands of holly and pine hung all around, filling the room with the scent of Christmas.

"I love my wand!" Mia said, waving it again to magic up two beautiful turtle doves cooing Christmas carols.

Charlotte waved her wand and produced an amazing feast, with heart-shaped cakes and dainty biscuits iced in pink and gold.

"Let's do something for the Secret

Princesses," she murmured to Mia. "To thank them for helping us."

Mia thought for a moment, her eyes falling on the silk stockings Princess Cara had sewn for the Secret Princesses. They were hanging all around the ballroom.

She waved her wand. Suddenly, every stocking bulged with presents!

"What's all this?" asked Alice, going over to the stocking with her name on it and taking out a gift.

"Open it and you'll see!" said Mia, smiling.

The Secret Princesses opened their presents.

"Oh, it's perfect!" exclaimed Alice, holding up a gold heart-shaped photo frame. It was engraved with the words *Love and thanks*

from Mia and Charlotte. Inside was the photo
Princess Kiko had taken in front of the advent
calendar. Mia and Charlotte had given one to
every princess.

"That reminds me," said Princess Sophie,
smiling. "You two need to come and see
another picture."

She led them upstairs to the Portrait Gallery,
where paintings of all the Secret Princesses
through the years lined the hallway. Between
a portrait of Alice singing into a microphone
and a picture of Florence and Esme – the
last two Friendship Princesses – hung a new
painting.

Mia and Charlotte's faces beamed out from
the frame. Princess Sophie had painted them

wearing their pink and gold princess dresses
and holding their pendants together to form
a heart.

"It's gorgeous!" said Mia.

"I love it!" said Charlotte, hugging Sophie.

Seeing their portrait hanging among
paintings of so many other amazing princesses,

Mia thought she might burst with pride.

Hand in hand, the girls returned to the ballroom with Sophie.

"Three cheers for our newest princesses," called Alice as they entered the room.

"HIP HIP HOORAY!" everyone shouted.

Then they danced and celebrated for hours, until Alice noticed Mia yawn.

"It's been a very long night," Alice said gently. "You should probably go home and get some sleep."

"But I don't want tonight to end," Charlotte protested. "I want to stay."

"Now that you're Secret Princesses, you don't need to wait for your pendant to glow," explained Alice. "You can wish to come back

189

to Wishing Star Palace whenever you like."

"Yay!" squealed Mia and Charlotte.

"I hope all your Christmas wishes come true," Alice said, hugging them each goodbye.

"They already have," said Mia, hugging her back.

"Merry Christmas, Princess Mia," said Charlotte, grinning at her best friend.

"And to you, Princess Charlotte," said Mia, beaming.

Together, they clicked the heels of their ruby slippers together three times and called out, "Home!"

As the magic carried Mia back to her house, she couldn't stop smiling. It wasn't even Christmas yet, but she'd already received the best present imaginable. She could come back to Wishing Star Palace whenever she wanted – to grant wishes with Charlotte! Their training was over, but their Secret Princess adventures were just beginning!

The End

Find out how Mia and Charlotte's adventure began!

Read on for a sneak peek!

The Magic
Necklace

Mia and Charlotte hugged each other.
"I don't want to go," whispered Charlotte,
her eyes stinging with tears.

"I don't want you to, either," said Mia
bravely. "But we'll always be best friends.
No matter how far apart we are."

"Always," promised Charlotte.

As they hugged, there was a knock at the door. The girls looked at each other in surprise.

"Come in!" called Mia. A beautiful older girl with strawberry-blonde hair streaked with bright red opened the door. She was wearing a short denim skirt and sparkly sandals. On her white top rested the necklace she always wore, a gold pendant shaped like a musical note, so shiny that it almost seemed to glow.

"Alice!" Charlotte and Mia gasped, jumping to their feet.

Their pop star friend looked incredibly glamorous, but her smile was just as warm as ever. "Your mums are looking for you.

I thought I might find you up here."

They ran over and hugged her. "How come you're back?" Mia said.

"Your mum emailed me about the party and I really wanted to come. I'm only here for a few hours, though. I have to travel up north for a concert I'm doing tomorrow night, but I just couldn't let Charlotte go to California without saying goodbye," Alice said. "I can't believe you're moving."

"I know," said Charlotte.

They all sat down on the bed together. Despite feeling miserable about leaving, Charlotte couldn't help but smile as she looked at Alice. It was so nice to see her again. "I'm so glad you could come."

Alice squeezed her hand. "So why aren't you two downstairs dancing?"

Mia swallowed. "We didn't feel like it."

Alice's blue eyes softened. "I know it's hard, but you can still be best friends even if you're far apart."

"It's just not going to be the same," said Charlotte, sighing. "We won't be able to see each other much at all."

Alice looked from one girl to the other. "Maybe you will."

"What do you mean?" asked Charlotte in surprise.

Alice smiled mysteriously and pulled something out of her pocket. It was a golden necklace. "Charlotte and Mia," she murmured. She closed her hand for a moment and waved her other hand over it.

When Alice opened her hand again, there were two necklaces nestled in her palm!

"How ... how did you do that?" stammered Mia, astonished.

Alice jumped to her feet. "There isn't time to explain right now. Just remember this ..." She handed them each a necklace. "Wishes *do* come true. As long as you keep each other in your hearts, you'll never be alone. Now, quick – put the necklaces on!"

Charlotte fastened the necklace she was holding around Mia's neck, then Mia did the same for her. As soon as the necklaces were around their necks there was a tinkling sound and a bright flash of light.

"Oh my gosh!" said Charlotte. A pendant in the shape of half a heart had appeared on Mia's necklace. Charlotte looked down and gasped. Hanging from her own necklace was a pendant just like Mia's!

Mia's eyes were wide as she stared in amazement. "But … but that's impossible!" she whispered as she looked at the beautiful half-heart pendant.

"Not impossible – magic!" Alice said softly, before hugging them both. "I knew you two were special!" she said mysteriously.

Mia gently lifted her pendant and held it against Charlotte's. Together, they formed a perfect heart. Mia's hand tingled as the heart began to glow, filling her bedroom with warm, bright light. She was so excited she could barely breathe.

"Charlotte! Mia! Come down or you'll miss the whole party!" Charlotte's mum called from downstairs, breaking the spell. Startled, the girls dropped their pendants and they stopped glowing.

The girls looked at each other in amazement. But before they could ask Alice any questions, she grabbed their hands and smiled. "Come on, let's dance together while we still have a chance!" And with that, they all ran downstairs.

Read *The Magic Necklace* to find out what happens next ...

Secret Princesses Quiz

Yay! Mia and Charlotte have earned their wands and become Secret Princesses. Have you been following their journey every step of the way? Take this quiz to find out if you are a Secret Princesses expert.

1. What lets Secret Princesses travel magically from one place to another?

A. Ruby slippers
B. Diamond tiaras
C. Moonstone bracelets

2. Which Secret Princess wears a necklace with a pawprint pendant?

A. Princess Sylvie
B. Princess Phoebe
C. Princess Ella

3. Who gave Mia and Charlotte their magic necklaces?

A. Princess Kiko
B. Princess Alice
C. Princess Cara

4. How many turrets does Wishing Star Palace have?

A. Three
B. Four
C. None

5. Which Secret Princess bakes magical treats?

A. Princess Sylvie
B. Princess Sophie
C. Princess Anna

6. What colour light comes out of Princess Poison's wand?

A. Black
B. Silver
C. Green

7. Where does Charlotte's family live?

A. England
B. California
C. Australia

8. What did Mia and Charlotte earn for granting four watery wishes?

A. Sapphire rings
B. Moonstone bracelets
C. Aquamarine combs

9. What is Mia's little sister called?

A. Elsie
B. Flossie
C. Evie

10. Which Secret Princess is a talented artist?

A. Princess Luna
B. Princess Grace
C. Princess Sophie

Answers: Give yourself one point for every question you got right.

1. A
2. C
3. B
4. B
5. A
6. C
7. B
8. C
9. A
10. C

Scores

0-3 Oh dear! You need to brush up on your Secret Princesses knowledge.

4-6 Good effort! There might be some Secret Princesses books you haven't read yet.

7-10 Amazing! You are a Secret Princesses expert, just like Mia and Charlotte!

How to Hold a Bake Sale

Mia and Charlotte help Kat and Shelley
run a bake sale to raise money for the prom.
Bake sales are a great way to raise money for
a good cause. Here's what you need to do ...

Before the Bake Sale

1. Decide on a time and a place. School is a great place to hold a bake sale, but you will need to ask for permission first.

2. Make posters advertising the bake sale and asking people to bake or buy treats. Hang them up where lots of people will see them.

3. Find volunteers to help you on the day of the sale.

4. With a grown-up's help, bake yummy treats to sell. Brownies, biscuits and cupcakes are all good choices.

On the Day

1. Set up a table and add a tablecloth to make it look nice. Then lay out all the treats people have donated.

2. Make price labels and put them in front of each type of treat.

3. Use a plastic tub or tin as a money box and be sure to have plenty of change.

4. Make sure your hands are clean when serving your customers.

5. Thank every customer for supporting a good cause.

6. Tidy up when the sale is done.

7. Give the money you raised to charity.

Top Tips from Princess Sylvie
- List each cake's ingredients in case any customers have food allergies.
- Don't forget to provide paper plates and napkins.
- Bunting, doilies and cake stands will make your cake sale look great.

Secret PRINCESSES

What would you wish for?

Are you a Secret Princess?

Join the Secret Princesses Club at:

secretprincessesbooks.co.uk

Explore the magic of the
Secret Princesses and discover:

♥ Special competitions! ♥
♥ Exclusive content! ♥
♥ All the latest princess news! ♥